MW01223648

THE CHEADLES

by

Christobel Cook

authorHOUSE®

AuthorHouse™ UK Ltd.
500 Avebury Boulevard
Central Milton Keynes, MK9 2BE
www.authorhouse.co.uk
Phone: 08001974150

First published by AuthorHouse 9/26/2007

ISBN: 978-1-4343-2512-9 (sc)

Printed in the United States of America
Bloomington, Indiana

This book is printed on acid-free paper.

Contents

Chapter One: The Cheadles

The fair was coming to town! The children were very excited, all chattering at the same time.

I want to go on the Noah's Ark, " said Peggy loudly;

"And the bumper cars, " cried George,

"Stop it ….stop it at once" shouted Sally. "It's like bedlam in here, no one will go to the fair if you do not quieten down; anyway it doesn't start until Saturday, and you will have to wait and see what your dad says. Now get ready for tea; he will be home soon and he will want a bit of peace and quiet."

Sally and Joe Cheadle had four children; Fred the eldest was eleven; Mary ten; Peggy seven, and the youngest, George was four. Although they didn't have much money, they were a very happy clean living family. The house they lived in was very old with no modern facilities at all. Although it had three bedrooms they were quite small, but Sally with the help of her eldest daughter Mary managed to keep the bedrooms reasonably tidy. The house did not have a bathroom but with the aid of an old tin bath, which they kept in the brick wash house, in the back yard, they all had a weekly bath, usually on a Friday night. The yard also housed the water tap and was shared with the house next door. The lavatory was also in the yard but of course had no flushing water it held a bucket under the seat, which had to be emptied right down the end of the garden in a very large cesspit, of cause this was Joe's task twice weakly.

Sally and her eldest would sit in the evenings cutting up squares of newspaper to hang on a hook in the toilet; it was kept immaculately clean, as Sally would scrub the wooden seat every day.

Sally baked all her bread in the kitchen on a well scrubbed white wooden table and cooked on a large black range. It was always kept shiny with black lead and elbow grease. One side of the fire had a large oven with a shelf and on the other side was a small deep well for heating water. The kettle and saucepans went on the top of the fire or oven but nine times out of ten both. Joe always made sure Sally had plenty of water in the buckets before going off to work so she could top up the well as she used the hot water. Sally had a big ladle to get the water out with, of course the children were not allowed to use it in case they scolded themselves.

Friday nights they all had a bath in front of the fire, the bath held a lot of water so Sally would start with the youngest and add more hot for the next one. The two eldest children bathed and saw to themselves, they needed a bit of privacy now they were older.

Joe and Sally would have their bath when the children were all tucked up in bed. Whilst Joe was having his bath Sally was tidying up and making sure the children were asleep. She went to the girl's room first, they were fast asleep, she gently kissed them on the cheek and blew out the candle. George was asleep but Fred was trying to read.

"Come on now son you will hurt your eyes in this light", she spoke softly so as not to disturb George.

"Okay mum", he whispered back, "goodnight and God bless"

"Goodnight son, sleep well"

She realised her eldest son was almost a man now, his voice was deeper and he was very aware of himself. He was very careful not to undress in front of Sally, or the other children for that matter. She came quietly down the stairs and sat in the big armchair by the side of the fire. Joe sat in the other chair opposite.

They had gas mantles down stairs, which gave a little more light than the candles upstairs. Even so, Sally never did any sewing at night, although sometimes she would read a book, but only for a short period at a time, and only if Joe was reading the newspaper. Mostly they liked to talk over the day's events.

"You know Joe", Sally said, "Our Fred is almost a

man now, don't you think it's time to have a talk with him".

Joe laughed; "Good God Sal; I bet he could tell me a thing or two, unless he has got his head buried in the sand, Now!.......Now!....; don't fret yourself girl. I will have a talk with him, you needn't go in a huff."

"I'm not in a huff," she said sitting up straight in her chair. It was a high back chair with wooden arms, but had a nice thick cushion, so it was very comfortable

Joe rose from his armchair and lay down on the rug in front of the fire. It was a big rug of many colours, Sally had made it herself out of old stockings and such like. It was a lot of work dyeing and cutting the materials into strips, which was then woven onto sacking cloth, with a hook on the end of a wooden peg. She had spent hours each day for weeks to get it finished, and was very proud of the end product.

Joe looked tenderly at Sal and said softly; "Come down here lass and have a cuddle with me, It's been a long time Sal."

"I know dear," she answered with the same tenderness, "but we really can't afford to have another baby, we can hardly make ends meet now."

"I promise you my dear I will be careful, I'm not a complete fool you know, just a hungry one." He looked at Sal pleadingly, he knew she would not refuse him.

Sal was very lucky really, as Mrs Jones, who lived down the lane, was beaten when she resisted her man. She often had to wear dark glasses to hide her black eyes. Sal wondered why she put up with it, she already had eight children and another on the way. Although she was having a difficult pregnancy her husband still never left her alone. He drank heavily especially on a Friday night after he had been paid his wages. Sex seemed to be his only other pleasure.

Sal looked at Joe lovingly and knew what a lucky woman she was. Joe was so kind and gentle, but very much a man. They had fallen in love at a very early age; her mother had called it "puppy love". There had never been another man in Sally's life at all, she had been a shy girl and very innocent. Her work mates would tease her by saying; "you know what you will have engraved on your tomb stone, (returned unopened). Sally would laugh with them but underneath it all, she was half-afraid it would be true.

Then Joe had proposed! What a magical evening that was. They were sitting in the park on a metal bench; Joe had put his arms around her and kissed her long and tenderly. To Sally time had stood still and she experienced all sorts of strange and wonderful feelings.

"What are you smiling at darling," said Joe, "you were deep in thought then weren't you?"

She smiled and slid softly to the floor to lay beside Joe in the comfort of his arms. He turned the gas mantle down low, but the light from the kitchen range was warm and relaxing the glow from the coals dancing excitedly through their hair giving a golden tinge to Sally's hair, and Joe's, black and shiny like silken threads. They just lay for a while wrapped in each other's arms watching the flames as they licked and caressed the chimney breast.

"I love you Mrs Cheadle," Joe whispered in Sally's ear as he penetrated her body, his movements firm but gentle.

They lay still for a while still locked in each other's embrace. Joe knew Sally was worrying; he held her tight reassuring her that it would be alright.

"Look darling," he said, holding up a little square packet, I was wearing a sheath; I had enough coppers to buy a packet of three; so you see you have nothing to worry about. But I must say it was like washing your feet with your socks on" They both laughed and the fear and tension disappeared from her face.

Chapter Two

Sal jumped out of bed "Come on Joe," she said with urgency in her voice; "you will be late for work," They woke up with such a start and realized they had overslept, she gave Joe a shake and leapt out of bed … "you won't have time for breakfast this morning; It's a good thing I did your lunch box last night…. I will do your flask whilst you swill your face…but do hurry Joe."

Joe worked at the local shoe factory; he was an experienced clicker. Old man Philips had taught him when he was just thirteen years old. Joe liked the work and he liked the men he worked with. Over the years he had worked in most of the rooms in the factory, but he preferred the clicking room. He found it very interesting cutting out the different designs and making new patterns. He had to concentrate on his work as it was all cut by hand and the tools and knives were very sharp. He knew how many uppers he could get out of one skin just by looking at it.

Joe was very popular, not only with the men, but also the women and young girls in the closing room; where the sewing of the uppers was done, they were always teasing him, in a very nice way, and he never took umbrage at anything they said to him.

Unusual for Joe; he walked in the factory ten minutes late, puffing and panting, where he had hurried up the hill. There were cries of ………..

"Aye…aye…Joe, what were you up to last night?"

"Did she tire you out then?" said another.

Joe just laughed at them and went straight to his bench. He had only been there for about an hour, when the manager sent for him to go to his office, which caused more comments and teasing.

"Who's been a naughty boy then?" said his best

mate Dick; "oh shut up man," said Joe playfully as he walked passed him to go to the office. Joe knocked on the door and walked in saying; "you wanted to see me Mr. Lompton".

"Yes Joe, come in and take a seat".

Joe sat down in an old but comfortable chair, the woodwork was very well polished, and although the upholstery was of dark green velour; it was showing signs of being well worn. Mr. Lomptons office was not overlarge, but nice and bright; as there was a large window, that overlooked the street and a few houses.

Beyond these the view was beautiful; nothing but fields of different shades of green, some dotted here and there with cows or sheep, it was very relaxing. In the summer months, when the trees were in full bloom there would often be children playing ball games while the mothers prepared the picnic. Joe sighed! he almost wished he could sit in this office...but would he get any work done! he thought to himself.

Mr. Lopton was always busy, Joe wondered if he ever

noticed all the beauty just outside his window. Joe felt quite sorry for him really, as he seemed such a lonely sort of man, since he had lost his wife and only child in a fire. That had been a dreadful time, and only two years ago. Mr. Lompton had been badly burned himself trying to save them both.

"Well Joe", he said, "I won't keep you long and I will come straight to the point; I have decided to retire early",

Joe couldn't conceal his surprise and made a little gasping noise.

"Yes I know it must be a shock to you, but since I lost my wife and daughter I don't feel I belong here, as you may have noticed Joe I don't make friends easily; so I have decided to go back to Scotland to be with my parents. They are getting on a bit now, and I feel I could do more good, looking after them. I've already put my house up for sale and started making plans....Well enough of that Joe....why I asked you to come to my office was to offer you my job, I have been following your progress for some time now and I am sure you will make a good manager. The men like and respect you, and you know the products from start to finish.

On Monday I would like you to start here with me for a month to learn the paper work and ordering of materials".

Joe sat very still in his chair as if mesmerized; he wasn't sure if he was dreaming or not, until the voice started again.

"We shall have to discuss your salary with Mr. Jackson of course, he already knows about it, and agrees that you are the man to take over from me…Well what do you say Joe?"

Joe couldn't believe what he was hearing; he had sat quietly listening with his mouth half-open.

"Well Mr. Lopton",he almost stammered, "of course…erm…I'm sorry to hear you are leaving; although I do understand why…erm.. at the same time I'm proud and delighted to be offered the job of manager.er..I..er..

I hope I can do it justice, as I'm not as educated as you". he smiled.

"If I didn't think you could do the job Joe, and do it well; I wouldn't be offering it to you" He spoke calmly and kindly as he always had a soft spot for this tall kind hearted man he had taught the trade too. He was a little rough around the edges, but Mr. Lopton had every faith in him.

"Would you like to talk it over with your wife tonight Joe; and give me your answer in the morning? as I would like to get it all settled as soon as possible."

"I will give you my answer now Mr. Lopton, I know what Sally would say; I accept your offer with the greatest of thanks".

They shook hands, and then Joe went back to the factory floor. The men of cause wanted to know why Joe was called to the office. Joe wanted Sal to be the first one to know the good news, so he bluffed his way round the question, not giving anything away.

By the time he reached home he was so full of excitement; he felt he would bust.

Sal cried with joy when she was told the good news; she was so happy for him, it was no more than he deserved, he was loyal and trustworthy and new every inch of the factory.

"You know what this will mean lass….we shall be able to rent a better house…One in Grundy street I should think…how does that sound?". His voice was full of excitement, "just think Sal, water on tap…a flush toilet…and electric light. No more emptying of buckets and emptying bath water from an old tin bath".

"Joe do stop it", Sal laughed, "it's too much….I can't take it all in". He wrapped his strong arms around her, and sweeping her off her feet, he swung her round and round until they were both giddy; Sal fell right on top of him, as Joe slithered to the floor.

That is how Fred found them when he came home from his paper round.

"Mum! Dad!" he shouted, "what would Peggy and George think if they had caught you at it?"

He was quite upset and obviously thought they were making love, if they had not been in such a happy mood, Sal knew that Joe would have been very angry, as he was always very careful where the children were concerned.

He knew he had to put Fred out of his misery, he playfully slapped Sal on the bottom and went upstairs. He knew Fred had gone to his bedroom, the lad always did when he was upset or he needed to be alone to think.

The staircase was very narrow and steep; also it had a nasty curve half way up. Fred was standing by the window when Joe went in, saying; "is it alright son if I come in? I need to talk to you….what you witnessed downstairs was not what you thought".

Joe told him all about the new job he had been offered, and what it would mean to them all. "Aw dad.. I'm sorry; but you must admit it did look bad," he laughed out loud, "sorry, I really am pleased about your new job…I hope we can move into Grundy street…that will make the kids at school sit up, I can just see their faces now."

Joe looked at his son tenderly and said; "how would you like to go to collage Son? And be somebody some day…maybe a doctor or a teacher, what do you think?"

"You know I want to be a blacksmith dad, I love being at the Smithy with Sam… he's teaching me how to shoe a horse dad, he knows everything about horses, and how to make things. I know it's dirty work, but oh dad I do love it. Sam said I could work with him when I leave school, and maybe take over one day. He's getting on a bit now you know dad, the other day he told me he was fifty five."

Joe didn't pursue the matter any further, but he knew Sal would be disappointed as he himself was. They both knew he had the brains and capabilities to do better than the smithy. Not that they had anything against Sam or his work, he was much needed in the villages around the area.

Joe came slowly down the stairs until he reached the curve, he then pulled himself up straight and put a smile on his face, he didn't want Sal to suspect anything wrong. He certainly didn't want to spoil the good news he had just brought home.

Chapter Three

The Cheadle family had been moved into 11 Grundy Street now for seven months and were well and truly settled in.

Fred had not changed his mind about becoming a blacksmith; in fact he was more determined than ever. He loved everything about it; the smell of burning hair when the horses were being shod.... And melting metal when tools were in the making. The shrill ring of the anvil conjured up all sorts of exciting feelings, as did the roar of the bellows when stoking up the fire. This was a job Fred loved; it gave him a feeling of power. In three more weeks Fred would be leaving school, and Mary would soon be waiting for her 11+ results. She was hoping she had passed for the girl's high school; she had worked so

Christobel Cook

hard, as she desperately wanted to become a teacher.

Although her parents were very proud of her, they had both secretly wished it had been Fred, they felt it was more important for a boy to be well educated; but they would not stand in Mary's way, if that is what she wanted to be.

Now Joe was manager of the shoe factory, they would be able to afford for Mary to go to collage later, if she still felt the same and did well. Everyone knew she was a clever girl, very studious. She always had her nose stuck in a book, (as her dad would say).

Peggy was the lively one, Mum always said she should have been a boy. She loved nothing better than playing football down the fields with the lads. Sal hoped she would grow out of it one day, and hopefully become more lady like, even if she wasn't as clever as her sister was.

Sal was a little worried about young Georgie these days, he was so thin and pale and had a continuous cough. He didn't seem to have much energy these days and often would fall asleep in the chair.

Two weeks before the end of half term Sal received a letter from the headmaster of the school George attended; asking her to go and see him.

"Good afternoon, Mrs Cheadle", the headmaster said as he extended his hand and shook her's gently, "please take a seat…I know we have not met before, but I feel sure you will know, my name is Mr. Blunt,….yes I do get a bit of stick about my name," He had obviously seen the amused smile creep over her face. "I am about to live up to it now though! I have had a report from George's teacher Mr. Black; he has brought to my attention that all does not appear to be all right with your son George. Twice this week he has fallen asleep at his desk. It has also been noticed that he is coughing a lot and the bouts are getting stronger….May I suggest a doctor is consulted!.. I don't wish to be rude but Mr. Black is most concerned about the boy."

There was a few minutes silence before Sal was able to speak, she was so taken back with Mr Blunts remarks, and felt so angry, she had momentarily been stunned into silence. However she tried hard to compose herself as she said, rather stiffly,

"I am sure there is no need for alarm Mr. Blunt; but I will certainly have the doctor check my son over. I will make an appointment to see him privately tomorrow, so I am afraid he will be absent from school,"

With this last remark she rose from her chair, shook hands with him politely, then opened the door saying, "I will inform you of the outcome of my visit to the surgery, gooday to you and thank you for your concern."

Sal did not go straight home, but went to the park close by, she sat quietly for half an hour thinking over all that had been said; also George's behaviour pattern over the last few weeks. On reflection, he had been coughing for some past few months now. She had not paid too much attention to it until recently; after all she had the other children to worry about too! Didn't she! she asked herself.

Sal began to feel a bit guilty… suppose there was

something wrong....it would be all her fault; had she really neglected him? . She asked herself these questions over and over until she thought her head would split in two from shear pressure.

Eventually Sal went home to an empty house, she kept herself busy by doing some ironing, it was such a chore, and yet made easier now she had an electric iron instead of that heavy old thing she used to heat on the fire; but it never stopped her mind from working overtime.

After the children were all in bed that night, Sal and Joe sat discussing the day's events; she had already made an appointment to see the doctor. They both knew in themselves something was not quite right with George. He used to be such a lively little boy and full of energy. They were both trying very hard not to show the panic they were feeling.

Doctor Cozen examined George very thoroughly and took a sample of his blood; he told them they would have to wait ten day's for the results of the tests. The doctor couldn't be quite certain, but he thought it was more than likely George would be admitted to hospital for a few days.

This piece of news upset Sal; the doctor could see panic written all over her face. "There is no need for you to look so distressed Mrs.Cheadle; it's just a precaution to make sure everything is in working order"; he smiled kindly at her. "In the meantime I would suggest you keep George away from school, and get him to rest as much as you can. Sal took notice of everything the Doctor said, and assured him George would have plenty of rest.

Luckily they didn't have to worry about medical bills, as they were all on the doctors panel, which meant Sally paid each week, something like an insurance policy really.

When they arrived home Sally made George a bed on the sofa, as she covered him with a blanket, he looked into her eyes and said quietly, "I'm going to die Mum aren't I?"

She looked lovingly at her youngest son, his eyes were sunken into a very pale face, although her heart was breaking, Sal tried to sound cheerful as she said; "Darling George; we are all going to die one day….but not just yet eh!… we have a lot of living to do first, so let's not hear anymore talk about dying".

"Okay Mum," George said cheering up a little, "when I'm a man, I'm going to look after you and Dad, cause you'll both be old then won't you?"

Sal burst out laughing; "The things you come out with Georgie you ought to be a comedian on the stage. How about you having a nap now while I start getting tonight's meal ready".

Sal went into the kitchen and peeled and chopped potato's carrots and onions and put them in a large earthenware dish, half filled it with water, sprinkled a few herbs from the garden, and laid fresh portions of chicken on the top, put the lid on and popped it in her nice new oven to slowly cook. She was very proud of her new cooker; in fact she was very proud of her home altogether. After her old home, it felt and looked like a palace to Sally.

Luckily the garden had been well maintained, she wasn't sure what all the herbs were, but a patch of the garden was well stocked with them. It was a large garden with a mixture of lawns and flowerbeds, with a stone path right down the middle. Her herb patch was right under her kitchen window.

George by now had fallen asleep, Sally looked at him and thought; he's such a small boy with his blonde curly hair and big blue eyes, or at least they were until he became ill. Now they looked dark and sunken into the back of his sockets. He had never been a big child but now he was painfully thin. His constant coughing was getting him down. Sally was afraid…of what? She wasn't quite sure.

Sally couldn't understand how a happy lively boy could deteriorate like this in such a short space of time. Had she neglected to notice the change in him? …..
When did she first notice it?.. She couldn't answer any of her own questions her mind was in such turmoil.

George slept for a good two hours until a sudden

bout of coughing woke him; it was a very nasty bout and took every ounce of energy out of him, and left him exhausted. Sal took him in her arms and tried to comfort him, but shortly followed another fit of coughing; but this time it was different, he was coughing up blood.

Fortunately Joe had had a telephone installed only two weeks ago, so Sally was able to phone the doctor and Joe right away. Her husband was home within minutes but the doctor was delayed. He was attending Mrs Cash who lived a few doors away; he had just delivered her third child.

When he arrived at the house and saw what the situation was, he lost no time in calling for an ambulance.

George was not taken to the hospital but to the sanatorium; Sal knew then that her first fears had been right, poor Georgie had consumption. Both Sally and Joe went in the ambulance; Sal had left a note on the kitchen table for Fred, asking him to look after Mary and Peggy and she would phone him later to explain.

The journey in the ambulance was long and painful as they sat beside their young son, holding his hand, and trying to comfort him. They were hurting inside and trying desperately not to let Georgie see the tears in their eyes

The Sanatorium was very busy; nurses were flitting here there and everywhere, but still managing to look calm and efficient. Everywhere looked scrupulously clean and clinical. The walls were all painted white, and the floors shone like glass, yet were not at all slippery.

Sister came down the passage to greet them; she wore a dark blue uniform with a little white cap perched cheekily on her head. She smiled at them saying in a clear soft voice; "you must be the Cheadle family, would you care to follow me please; I will show you to your sons bed. My name is Sister Green and I will be in charge of your sons welfare."

Once they had got George settled in his bed, Sister asked them if they would like a cup of tea, as it would be quite a while before the doctor would be free to see them.

There were five other beds in the ward occupied by five young lads, they all looked older than George, but they all seemed very friendly.

A tall slim man walked briskly down the ward, his white coat flapping at his sides where the buttons were left undone. His face was like a mask giving nothing away. He introduced himself to Sal and Joe; his voice was quite soft and deep. Rather pleasant Sal thought to herself.

He tried to put the situation as clearly as possible without alarming them too much. He wanted to do a lot more simple tests before he could confirm anything; but he would not keep them hanging on too long, as he knew what they must be going through.

Joe held Sal's hand tight; he could feel a slight trembling in her body, he hoped she wasn't going to faint. Her face had gone white like chalk. Joe felt so helpless, why was life being so cruel to them? George was such a good little boy, he hadn't been any trouble at all from the day he was born.

They both thanked the doctor, and as they rose to go, he took hold of Sally's hand and said;"Try not to let the boy see you are upset; you must be brave for his sake, he will cope if you allow him to". Sal shed a few tears before they went back to the ward. She knew people with consumption did not really get cured; she only hoped George would hang on as long as possible. He seemed too small to have much fight left in him; it didn't seem fair that one so young and innocent should have to suffer!…what was God thinking about! Sal was thinking all this while they were walking to the ward.

They finally left George quite happy talking to the other lads and made their way home. Luckily they didn't have to wait too long for a bus, they talked very little, holding hands tightly said it all.

The other children were very upset when told what was happening, especially Mary; she took the news very badly; it took all Sal's strength to console her as she was in such distress herself. But Mary was such a caring child and realised what the outcome would be.

Every afternoon Sal would catch the bus at the end of the road and go to the San, to see George. He appeared to be getting weaker and thinner as the months went by. Sal coped with the situation as best she could; and tried to appear cheerful in front of George. Little did he know her heart was breaking! How could he know, he was so young and desperately ill.

At night Sal would lay in Joe's arms and sob herself to sleep; but surely she must realise he was hurting too; who was comforting him?

Because of his work Joe could not visit his son everyday, but he spent as much time as he could at the weekends. Sometimes they would take the other children with them at the weekend. Sal did not mind Mary and Fred going but was a little concerned about Peggy seeing her young brother in this state.

Fred was almost grown up now; he was very understanding and helped his parents as much as he could; especially with the two girls. He would take Peggy to bed and tuck her in and read her a fairy story, before kissing her goodnight.

Sal looked at her eldest son lovingly and said;"Fred my boy, you will make someone a good husband and father one day" Fred only smiled. At this stage in his life Fred did not appear to be interested in girls, not in the sexual way at least. But his mother new it would not be long before he became aware of new inner feelings.

The night seemed long, as Sal lay awake thinking of Georgie and trying hard not to sob loudly. She thought Joe was asleep until his strong warm arms reached out and engulfed her in love and comfort. It was at that moment the floodgate opened and tears ran unabated down her face; "he's not going to make it is he Joe?

Joe couldn't speak he could only hold her even closer, their wet cheeks touching. Poor Joe was trying to be strong for both of them.

Two days later they were both sent for, as the doctor didn't think George could hang on for very much longer. He had deteriorated rapidly in the last few hours, his breathing was laboured and getting weaker.

Sal and Joe could only sit beside him each holding a tiny hand. They were both feeling helpless and heartbroken.

In the early hours of the morning, Georgie quietly slipped away from them all, his suffering drained from his face; he was at peace. Poor Sal was reluctant to let go of his hand; she had lost her little boy…her baby.

The whole family were devastated, but Joe had to show calm and understanding for the sake of the other children Fred was a tower of strength and helped cope with the everyday jobs while Sal and Joe saw to all the funeral arrangements. The vicar was very kind, he knew little Georgie very well, as the small child had been going to Sunday school from a very early age and had been very popular.

The morning of the funeral, the church was packed to its fullest capacity, it appeared the whole village had turned out to pay their respects. He was such a well loved little boy and very well behaved; the school would miss him dearly. Joe knew it would take him and his family a long time to come to terms with this tragedy especially his mother.

Sal and Joe had a wreath made of bronze chrysanthemums in the shape of a teddy bear and in its arms it was holding a tiny bunch of red rose buds. They received many sympathy cards and floral tributes, it was really unbelievable. The nurses from the hospital had sent a small cross of white and blue flowers and three of the nurses attended the funeral.

The hymns Sal had chosen were George's favourites….. All things bright and beautiful and …Jesus wants me for a sunbeam. He was always singing one or the other especially when he wanted to be noticed, if Sally was busy. She often joined in with him; but not today, the words stuck in her throat and were washed away with her tears.

Would they ever forget this day? Sal looked at the little coffin,…could her little boy really be in that….NO….. NO…it's not true, she wasn't sure if she had spoken the words aloud before she entered into oblivion.

Joe caught her as she was sliding off her seat; he didn't quite know what to do until someone behind handed him a bottle of smelling salts. He undid the top and wafted it under Sally's nose; which soon revived her.

Chapter Four

Six months on and Joe was still worried about Sal, he knew she spent all her spare time at the cemetery where George was buried. Was it really six months? It seemed like only yesterday since they were a laughing happy family.

On several occasions Joe had managed to slip away from the factory and observe Sal's behaviour, unbeknown to her. Sometimes she would just talk softly to her child, other times she would croon one of the lullaby's she sang to him when he was a baby. She had such a sweet voice; Joe would slink away unseen with tears in his eyes.

There was nothing he could do but be patient and hope that one day in the near future Sal would come to terms with her grief.

Fred was now working at the smithy with Sam, and Mary was doing well at the girls high school. Peggy wasn't such a tomboy these days; she had become quieter and more subdued. Sal wasn't so sure if this was a good sign or not. Peggy's moods changed, she was sultry and bad tempered most of the time; yet she could be loving and gentle at others. Poor Sal didn't know how to cope with her somedays; scolding seemed to make her more agitated than ever. Rather than do battle with her she would often send her to her room, but Sal was not happy doing this as she knew Peggy only lay on her bed and sobbed. If only she would tell me what is troubling her thought Sal, as obviously something was wrong, her behaviour wasn't normal.

Today she had been exceptionally difficult, and Sal had to slap her sharply across the face; she was quite hysterical. At that moment Fred had walked in from work, he had come home early, owing to a slight accident. A piece of coke had fallen off the fire and had just caught him on his foot. He thought Sam was making to much fuss by sending him home, as it wasn't that bad really, he had been very lucky.

When he saw the state Peggy was in he whipped her up in his strong arms, kicking and screaming and carried her upstairs to her room. He was so angry he almost threw her on the bed. He never said a word; he just walked out of the room locking her door behind him. He was anxious to get down stairs again to see if his mother was alright, he hoped Peggy would calm down if she was left locked in her room for a while.

He found his mother sitting at the kitchen table with her head on her folded arms, quietly sobbing, her shoulders heaving to the rhythm of her grief. She lifted her head when Fred spoke and looked at him with a tear stained face.

"How long has our Peggy been treating you like this mum?.. What on earth is it all about?.

"Hey one question at a time son," she smiled through her tears, "Peggy has been acting strange for quite a while now, I can't remember exactly when it first started or why; but I must admit she has never been as bad as this before."

She gave a deep sigh. "I suppose your dad will have to be told now. I've been avoiding it as long as possible in case he loses his temper with her. I'm sure it's some kind of help she needs. If only she would confide in me, I can't help if I don't know what the matter is. Sal turned to Fred and said," have you any suggestions son cause I'm at the end of my tether."

"I wonder if talking to her teacher would help mum; after all a lot of her time is spent at school, they may have noticed a difference in her behaviour. Anyway it's worth a try isn't it,?

" Yes son I think that would be a good move, or I could ask Dr. Cozen for a tonic for her. Anyway I will speak to her teacher first and take it from there."

When Joe arrived home, Peggy was still locked in her room. He knew at once something was wrong; he could smell the dinner cooking, but unusual for Sal the table was not laid out, ready for a meal. Sal and Fred were both sitting at the table looking very serious; he also noticed Sal's red eyes.

"What's going on Sal; and where are Mary and Peggy?" She looked at him and said in a soft voice, "Mary is at her friends house, Brenda's mother said she could stay the night, but Peggy is locked in her room" before she could say anymore Joe had noticed Fred's foot was bandaged up, he looked at him enquiringly.

Fred immediately responded with, "Oh don't worry about that dad, it isn't as bad as it looks. Sam insisted on bandaging it, you know how he is dad, an old fusspot." Fred laughed and a little of the tension in the room subsided.

That evening went very slowly, after dinner Sal crept upstairs to Peggy's room, when she unlocked the door and peeped in she found Peggy fast asleep clutching her old stuffed rabbit that Sal had made for her when she was a baby. She looked so young and peaceful, with her tear stained face, that it was hard for Sal to be cross with her. Sal thought to herself…. If only I knew what was bothering her, as obviously something was. She was sure it was nothing to do with her little brothers death, she seemed to have come to terms with that. Perhaps she would open up to Mary, they were very close.

Sal didn't wake her up; she thought sleep would do her good just now, let's hope and pray in the morning, things would be better she said to herself.

Mary arrived home at lunch time the next day, she was full of excited chatter, Mum can Brenda stay the night with us on Friday?"

"We will see dear, at the moment I am a bit worried about your sister, something is playing on her mind and she won't tell me what's troubling her. She suddenly can't change like this without a reason."

"Don't worry mum I will see if she will confide in me, is it okay if I take her to the park after dinner?" Sal was very grateful to her daughter, as she herself didn't seem able to get through to her.

Dinner went down quite smoothly, although a little quieter than usual. As they were about to leave the table Mary gave her mother a sly wink;

"Is it okay if I go to the park? I promise I will help

with the dishes later". Sal played along with her, "Our Mary you will make any excuse to get out of the washing up,..go on…but don't be too late home".

As she was about to go out the door, she turned to Peggy and said, "How about keeping me company Peggy? We can take the bats and a ball if you like"

Peggy at first looked as if she was going to say no, but then seemed to change her mind; although she wasn't very enthusiastic. The park was not very far away; they soon arrived to find all the swings were occupied. They weren't too bothered though, they made their way towards the sandpit.

There was a big expanse of grass close by where they could attempt a game of tennis. The game eased the tension between them, and soon they were laughing and enjoying themselves. When they were both out of breath, they found an empty bench where they could sit and recover.

"Do you think we will ever be good enough to play on the tennis courts", said Peggy. Mary laughed as she replied, "Of course in about ten years time. I'm glad we came here together Peggy, you haven't been too happy lately have you? Do you want to talk about it"?……….. "NO"…… Peggy said sharply.

"Sorry Peggy" Mary said in a soft voice, "I don't want to pry, but I thought if you had a problem I could perhaps help. I didn't get on very well with one of my teachers, but talking it over with Fred helped me a lot."

With this remark Peggy started to cry, Mary put her arm around her to give her comfort. Her young shoulders shook with her grief.

"I'm going to die Mary, just like Georgie did," Her outburst caught Mary by surprise "What ever gave you that idea Peggy?"

Peggy whispered, "I have been bleeding, not from my mouth but from the other end"

"Oh Peggy if only you had told me or mum before we could have saved you a lot of grief. What is happening to you happens to all girls when they start to mature;

you know; grow up. Its called having a period and it will happen every month. Are you bleeding now dear? I have some sanitary towels in my bedroom, I will make you a belt and show you how to use them".

"I'm alright now, it happened last week, I've hidden my dirty knickers under the bed". Peggy sounded so serious Mary had to stop herself from laughing, but instead she put her arms around her shoulders and said kindly,

"I think we had better go home now and have a chat with mum, she will explain more about it. But I want you to promise me that if anything bothers you, no matter what it is you will come and talk to me about it. It will save a lot of heartache. I would imagine a lot of the girls in your class have started their periods."

They walked home in silence, each deep in their own thoughts. Peggy realised now she would have to talk to her mother about her problem, and also to apologise for all the stress she had caused. She loved her mother very much and didn't mean to hurt her. Peggy new she would be forgiven, it seemed a load had been taken off her mind and she felt a lot happier inside.

Chapter Five

Joe came home with a very worried look on his face. Sal looked at him enquiringly, "Is something wrong at work Joe? you look troubled"

"No lass, no trouble at work, but I am concerned, your right there girl. It looks like we shall be at war before many more days are over" Sal put her arm around his shoulder as he sat down wearily in his armchair.

"You won't have to go to war Joe; will you?" There was a touch of fear in her voice.

"Not at first my dear, at my age they would have to be desperate" he tried to sound light-hearted, but he didn't fool Sal; not one little bit.

Joe turned the wireless on and sat listening to the

news, while Sal dished up the dinner; She called the rest of the family except Fred; he was still at the smithy. She put his plate in the oven, as she knew he would be home in a few minutes, so it wouldn't have time to dry up.

They ate the meal in silence, even the children seamed subdued. Fred arrived home before the meal was over, he guessed what they were all brooding about and tried to cheer them up; by telling them some of the amusing things that had happened at the forge. He told them one horse had flicked it's tail so hard, it had knocked his cap off his head. Mary and Peggy laughed so much they had tears running down their cheeks. Sal looked at her son and smiled her thanks for cheering the atmosphere.

He had the right qualities to make a good husband and dad one day. She knew he could be firm too, if necessary, but she had never seen him nasty, not even after he had had a drop too much to drink. Then he was lovey dovey and nostalgic one minute and giggly the next. But he never drank too much very often. By the weekend things were looking very grim.

Sunday September 3rd 1939 war was declared! Sal, Joe and Fred sat up very late discussing the situation. They both knew what was in Fred's mind before he even spoke!

"I know you won't like it mum, but I hope you will try and understand; I know dad will. I am going to enlist for the army; if they will have me. I shall be eighteen next month"

He heard his mother catch her breath, and saw her hand go up to her mouth. Fred sprang from his chair and went over to comfort her; he held her close, and knew she was crying inside, but was fighting the tears back.

It was quite a while before she spoke, and in a soft voice said; "You must do what you think is right son. I can only hope and pray for your safe return to us; we shall miss you" Joe and Fred were both taken back by her acceptance of his decision…. It was as if she had expected it!

"I knew you would understand mum;" he gently kissed her on her cheek.

He tried to be flippant as he joked, "just think of all those letters you will have to read, and how proud you will feel when you show your friends my photo", here he stood up straight and in a girlish voice, and pretending to hold a photo, he said, " This is my son in his uniform, doesn't he look handsome?" Fred looked and sounded so funny; the three of them ended up rolling about with laughter..

Joe patted him on the back playfully saying, "time for bed little soldier"

"Aw dad, not so much of the little, I'm a man now"

"Yes my son you are a man now," Joe replied with a sigh. They decided not to say anything to the girls just yet; they would know soon enough

There wasn't much sleep to be had that night, Sal, Joe, and Fred all had the same sort of thoughts running through their minds. Sal lay awake long after Joe had drifted off, the ticking of the old alarm clock sounded so loud in the still of the night, she could almost imagine it was bombs going off. She scolded herself severely; turned over on her side and closed her eyes. But sleep still didn't come easily.

Chapter Six

Ten days after his eighteenth birthday, Fred enlisted for the army; he was very excited, as he passed A1. Three other lads in the area also passed A1; Bill Scriber, Jack Timper and Dick Green. The four of them had been good mates ever since they had left school.

Bill was showing an interest in Mary, who had become a very attractive young lady. She however, did not appear to be aware of Bill in the same way, to her he was just a mate of her brothers.

The night before the boys had to report to Aldershot barracks; Bill plucked up courage to ask Mary if she would like to go for a walk with him.

She was taken back at first and was just about to say

no, when she caught her brothers eye. He seemed to be pleading with her to say yes, so dutifully she said, "okay Bill, I will just get my coat as I think it is a little chilly outside. I shan't be long mum"; she called as they went out of the door

They walked down the street and into the lane, which led to a little wooden bridge, that spanned the brook at the bottom of the lane.

Although it was usually dark at this time, tonight there was a moon that shone so brightly; it was almost like daylight. It was a beautiful night, the trees casting shadows and making all sorts of shapes and patterns. They walked over the bridge in silence, but when they reached the other end; Bill stopped and turned to face her and in a soft voice said; "Mary you know why I asked you out tonight don't you? I have thought a lot about you for sometime now; but I haven't plucked up enough courage to tell you" At this point he took hold of her hands; "Will you write to me while I'm away?"

"Of course I will Bill", she replied, a little too quickly,

as she was very embarrassed. She had never been out with a boy before or at least not like this and she wasn't quite sure how to handle the situation

Bill pulled her close to him and put his arms around her, he seemed to sense her nervousness and said gently; "It's okay Mary I wouldn't harm or frighten you... I respect you too much, but I would dearly love you to be my girl friend"

He kissed her softly on her lips, although his body was aching for something more. He knew he had to be careful or he would lose her altogether, he couldn't risk that happening. Besides Fred would thump him if he tried anything on.

Mary felt her whole body glow with warmth and started to relax a little. A grown up boy had never kissed her before, only her brother and it felt entirely different she thought to herself

She became aware Bill was talking to her, "Oh I'm sorry Bill, what were you saying?"

He looked serious now. " I know you are only sixteen Mary, but I do like you a lot. Will you write to me while I'm away in the army? I promise I will write to you" He sounded like a little boy asking for sweeties, she wanted to laugh, but she managed to control her emotions, after all, she didn't want to hurt his feelings.

"Of course I will write to you; you must tell me all about life in the army, and I will tell you about;" here she hesitated, she had almost said school, "Um…Um things happening here" she stammered.

"It's alright my love, I do know you are still at school" They both laughed and the tension was broken.

They walked slowly back to the house, Bill holding her hand. Mary was not quite sure how she should be feeling, she only knew it pleased her. But even so Mary felt sure love should be a little more exciting than just pleasant. Bill kissed her again before they eventually went into the house.

Fred looked at Bill with a grin on his face; "Everything okay mate?"

Mary went straight into the kitchen, where her mum was busy making a cup of tea; she looked up, "Oh hello dear, how did your walk go?"

"Okay mum, Bill has asked me to write to him, and be his girlfriend, do you think I should?" Sal thought for a second and then said, "Of course dear you are very young, but I don't really see any harm in you writing to one another. It doesn't mean you have to get serious does it? I dare say letters mean a lot to soldiers when they are away from home and their loved ones".

Not much happened in the next few weeks, Sal, and women like her, had been ordered to work. All the young and middle aged women who had no invalids, disabled, or pre-school children to look after, had to work in the munition factories, or other war effort occupations.

Sal was lucky; she was able to work in the shoe factory where Joe was the general manager, as they were now making army boots. She was quite happy to work in the closing room, although it was a lot different to dressmaking. She was used to a sewing machine so it wasn't too difficult to adjust to the different materials. The women she worked with were very friendly, it amused her when Joe came into the room, as it was obvious some of the women were sweet on him, and Joe didn't even notice. Sal would tease him about it when they were home.

Next year Mary would be sitting her exams for the teacher training collage, Sal hoped the war wouldn't spoil anything, as Mary had worked really hard. She knew she would not be fully qualified until her twenty first birthday, but she was prepared to work hard and achieve her goal. Hopefully one day maybe headmistress!...who knows!

As the war progressed, things were getting tougher and tougher, but Sal kept the family as happy as was possible. Mary had now gone away to collage, and Fred had been posted overseas, their was only herself, Joe, and Peggy at home.

The evacuees had started to arrive from London, poor little mites thought Sal and immediately volunteered to take some of them into her home, as after all she had got room now. The authorities allocated her three children, as they did not want to split any families up if it could be avoided. Sal didn't mind; poor little souls, there were two little girls and a boy.

The boy, named Harry was the eldest; he was eight, with the mind of a sixteen-year-old, what he didn't know about life was no body's business, yet his schoolwork was not good at all. He was rather a brash boy, with very dark eyes, that seemed to look right through you. Sal wasn't sure if she could handle him, but she was determined to try.

The two little girls were quite sweet, especially Betty, she was the youngest, not quite six, she had long blonde hair and bright blue eyes. It was hard to believe Harry was the brother of these two, as Hilda was as blonde as Betty was, also with grey blue eyes. She was seven and had nervousness about her.

Sal greeted them with a hug and a smile and said kindly; "Don't be afraid children, you will be quite safe here with us and we will try and make your stay a happy one. I expect you would like to see where you are sleeping. Well, I have put you girls together; but I thought you Harry, would like a room to yourself."

"Blimey"…gasped Harry… "I ain't ever 'ad a room to meself afore. It'll be like a toff, shall I 'ave to wear 'jarmers' like toffs do?" He pulled a funny face as he said this; Sal laughed and took them upstairs to their respective rooms.

When Sal saw the expression and wonder on their faces, her heart went out to them. It was obvious they had come from a poor family. She helped them unpack their few belongings and put them neatly away in the draws and wardrobe. There was not very much to hang up at all. Sal showed them where the bathroom was, then left them to look around and get used to their surroundings.

"My youngest girl Peggy will be from school soon, you will like her! She will be taking you three to school, as I have to work in the factory close by. I help to make boots for the soldiers to wear," she said this with a lot of pride in her voice.

When Peggy arrived home from school, the children were still upstairs in their room; "Hello mum, have they arrived yet?" she called out, as she opened the door.

"Shush dear, they will hear you", but Sal was smiling as she spoke, "They are still upstairs and very quiet....I wonder if they have fallen asleep?"

"What are they like mum?" Peggy asked excitedly, Sal laughed, "I think you are in for a treat; or shock dear, I'm not quite sure which yet. Creep upstairs Peggy just in case they have fallen asleep, tea will be ready as soon as your dad comes in."

Peggy went as quietly as she could up the stairs and stood in amazement, this strange little boy of eight was walking round the bedroom in bare feet; but it was the way he was walking! It reminded Peggy of someone running their fingers through their hair, was he looking for something he'd dropped! she thought to herself.

" I'm sorry," she said as she saw the little boy jump, and she saw such fear in his eyes, "I didn't mean to startle you. I'm Peggy and I guess you must be Harry, I do hope you will like living with us."

Harry just stood like a stuffed dummy and stared hard at her. Peggy was not quite sure what to say next, so she said the first thing that came into her head.

"Do you like the feel of the carpet on your toes? It has such a long soft pile on it hasn't it? This used to be little George's room you know; he was our youngest brother, but he died when he was very young…..from consumption"

Harry's face began to twitch as he said roughly, "Cor blimey I'm sorry"

"That sounds like dad is home", said Peggy as they heard the door handle downstairs rattle, "Come on, come downstairs and meet him, I know you will like him everybody does."

Harry hesitated, "does he wear a belt"

"Of course he does sometimes," Peggy laughed, "you are funny Harry, where are your sisters? We will go down together and meet dad"

The two girls were very excited, but Harry was very reluctant to go down. All the greetings over, they all sat down at the table, where Sal dished up a lovely meal for them all.

Harry ate everything that was put in front of him, as if there was no tomorrow, Hilda and Betty only picked at their meal, but Sal put this down to the upset of having to leave their parents.

That night when Joe had locked up and was climbing the stairs, he heard soft little sobbing noises coming from the girls' room. He peeped inside and discovered it was Betty crying into her pillow. She sounded so unhappy; Joe's heart immediately went out to her. He cradled her in his arms, rocking backwards and forwards, murmuring softly; "hush….sh; it's alright dear, everything will be alright; you will be safe with us. Sh…sh"

It wasn't long before she fell asleep, still cuddled up in Joe's arms. He laid her gently back down in the bed and tucked her in; kissing her softly on her cheek

Joe tiptoed along the landing to the bedroom he

and Sal shared; it was a lovely room with wall to wall carpeting in a shade of cream. The whole room was done out in different shades of pinks and creams. Sal was very proud of it. Joe's promotion had given them so much. They didn't have to struggle quite so hard when any bills came through the door, which was a blessing they both enjoyed.

Joe stood just inside the bedroom door; looking at Sal as she lay there, his heart was full of love, he crept into bed and lay beside her, he was longing to take her in his arms and make love to her. "Oh why did she have to fall asleep so quickly!" But Joe knew although his body ached for her he would not disturb her sleep.

Chapter Seven

The children had been living with the Cheadle family now for three months The two girls had settled down well, both at home and at school; but alas! Harry, he was a different kettle of fish. He didn't seem to stay out of trouble two days running, he enjoyed getting up to mischief especially at school or with the neighbours. Sal was unhappy about having to correct and punish him each day, she so wanted the children to love her; but how could Harry love her if she was always telling him off.

She was worried about him, and wondered why he was so different to the girls. It was hard to believe they were from the same family. Sal made up her mind to have a couple of hours off from work, so she could go and talk to the welfare officer who had allocated the children to her. She felt she needed some kind of help or advice. She knew Joe wouldn't approve, so she said nothing to him, or Peggy, about her intentions.

The waiting room at the welfare was very dingy, the paint was peeling off the doors, and the hard wooden chairs were most uncomfortable; there was nothing bright and cheerful about it at all.

Sal waited twenty minutes before an elderly lady called her name,

"Mrs Cheadle, Mrs Polter will see you now, will you kindly go to room one, just beyond

the door" Sal smiled at the little lady and made her way to the room as directed. When Sal entered the room, a very tall lady warmly greeted her and shook her hand.

"Please take a seat Mrs Cheadle, and how can I help you?"

Sal sat in the chair opposite Mrs Polter, who sat behind a well-polished desk. "I will come straight to the point Mrs Polter, I have come for a little advice on one of the evacuee children I have in my care; it's the boy Harry I am concerned about"

Mrs Polter smiled broadly, "Oh yes...Harry" she did not sound at all surprised; I I think I had better explain his position in the family, then you will perhaps understand why he is so different to the girls. You see, his mother had him before she was married, It wasn't too bad until the first girl of the marriage was born. Her husband then resented Harry and started to treat him rough. Harry had to learn how to be crafty and deceitful just to survive. Mr Prince was always telling him he was a bastard (excuse my language), and quite regularly took his belt off to him." Sal could not contain herself; she spoke before Mrs Polter could say anymore; " So that's what he meant when he asked Peggy if Joe wore a belt; poor boy" she said almost to herself. "Um yes" Mrs Polter went on, "his mother tried to protect him as much as she could, but every time she intervened he husband would beat her black and blue. The boy was kept in his room whenever Mr Prince was at home, but it was only a box room with a camp bed in it and cold lino on the floor."

Sal was almost in tears as she listened, "Thank you Mrs Polter, I can understand a lot of things now, but what I can't understand is, if the welfare knew all this why haven't they done anything about it?"

"Yes my dear I thought you might ask that question, but as a matter of fact it came to our attention two days before the children were evacuated. The authorities are looking into the matter now. After the war I don't think Harry will be going back to them, the girls will, as they are not at risk in anyway. I really should not have told you that Mrs Cheadle, I do hope however you will honour my confidence."

"Of course", Sal responded quickly, "but would you please inform me of any new developments, as I would like to take Harry into my home permanently. If I were to ask my husband and family I know they would feel the same as myself."

"I'm afraid Mrs Cheadle it isn't quite as simple as that, you see Harry and the girls are only here for the duration of the war, it is really up to head office. But I will certainly let the appropriate authorities know your feelings on the matter.

Sal made her way slowly back to the factory, she didn't appear to be in any hurry, she was churning over all that had been said. She could certainly understand some of Harry's bad behaviour, but not quite all. She was totally confused and upset, she somehow had to try and remove some of the bitterness and anger from Harry's young mind!... But how?

She would have to tell Joe about her meeting with Mrs. Polter, but of course no one else, it was imperative it was kept between the three of them, at this stage

On Saturday afternoon Joe took Harry to the pictures, as the boy had never seen a film before. Being a cowboy film Joe thought he would enjoy it, he wanted so badly for Harry to like and trust him.

Sal took the girls shopping and into a café for a milk shake after, so they all had an enjoyable day. The two girls were thrilled with the new clothes Sal bought them; she had also bought some new underwear and socks for

Harry.

Harry was over the moon and could talk about nothing else but Roy Rogers and Trigger, the horse. "Cor Aunt Sally, you should 'ave seen it, it was a whopper I aint never seen an 'orse do all them things afore"

Chapter Eight

Monday morning started off much the same as usual, Sal got the children ready for school, then off to work she went. Joe had been gone a couple of hours ago. He liked to be there to greet his pals good morning, his friendship with his pals had not changed when he was promoted, after all he said, he was still the same bloke, that hadn't changed.

Sal was working on her machine when the tragedy struck! There was an almighty thud, it was so loud and fierce the whole building shook and glass from the windows shattered everywhere, "Quick girls get under the benches and lie on the floor" shouted the foreman. But alas! Under the window where Sal's machine was, ran the hot water pipes. Luckily Sal was able to move quickly before she was too badly scolded. "Oh Sal, look at your arm", said one of her workmates, Sal was so much in shock she hadn't realised her arm was so red and swollen.

Someone shouted, "The school has been hit" The school was situated just across the other side of the road to the factory.

"My God, the children" Sal was right beside herself with fear, and before anyone could stop her, she fled from the factory and across to the school. By this time she was half-crying and half talking to herself. "I must find the children...please God let them be safe" she kept repeating it over and over.

The school was in a terrible state, glass and rubble everywhere, half of the building had gone. Sal searched frantically through the remaining classrooms. Parents children and teachers were milling around, they all appeared to be in a dazed state of shock. As parents found their children there was fresh tears flowing, from shear relief.

Sal was almost hysterical; no one seemed to have seen

her children…What on earth was she going to do! She went into the playground, or what was left of it. There was a whopping great hole right in the centre and half of the walls were down in a heap of rubble. She could see books and pencils, rubbers and even a little shoe, everywhere was a shambles; she felt sick to the bottom of her stomach.

After what seemed an eternity, she spotted Betty and Hilda cuddled close together in a corner; terror was written all over their faces. When Sal shouted their names, they ran quickly towards her, sobbing, and wrapping their arms around her waist. They clung to her as if stuck with glue, sobbing even louder.

"Pl..Please take us home mummy," Betty cried, Sal picked her up in her arms and tried to comfort her,then she put her down and picked up Hilda.

"Now darlings" Sal said, trying to pull herself together for the sake of the children, "Have you seen Peggy or Harry?" The two little girls shook their heads and held on tightly to Sal's hands; as if they were afraid she would go away and leave them.

The three of them waded through the rubble that was once the playground, going through the air-raid shelters. Sal was shouting frantically, "Peggy… Harry, has anyone seen Peggy and Harry?"

After what seemed a lifetime to Sal, she caught sight of Peggy; she was helping a teacher. They were both digging through the rubble with their bare hands. Sal clamped her hand over her mouth to stop herself from screaming, she had a frightened feeling in the pit of her stomach, she knew something was wrong…..Very wrong!

A voice in her head kept saying over and over…. No…No…not Harry … Please dear God.. Not Harry, She pulled herself together and told the girls to stay where they were, as she rushed forward to help Peggy and the teacher.

At first Peggy didn't even realise it was her mother helping, as she ordered her to remove some of the rubble away. Sal did not flinch; she just followed the order.

Two or three more stones revealed one very small hand and arm, "Quick" shouted Peggy; "move some more stones", but the stones were very large pieces of concrete and bricks, and they were very heavy. After much heaving and shoving they managed to remove most of them from the surrounding area.

They found the hand belonged to a little girl who was dead, but holding on to her other hand was another child; who was alive; but only just.. The teacher called for a stretcher and in response two young lads came running; carrying a mattress from the games room.

The teacher and Peggy between them, gently laid the small boy on the mattress, and told the lads to carry him carefully to the first aid post, that had been set up by the headmaster of the school.

One of the lads took off his jacket and gently laid it over the young boy, it was at this point, Sal realised the lad who took off his jacket, was Harry. Before she could speak, the ground came up and hit her.

Sal had never fainted in her life before, but it had

been such a shock and relief to see Harry was alive, and actually helping with the rescue; in his own small way. His little hands and face were covered in dust and sweat, she hardly recognised him. Harry himself was so absorbed in what he was doing, he didn't know it was Sal that had fainted, so he carried on with the job in hand.

When Sal came round, she was not quite sure if it had been Harry she saw at all. Maybe she had imagined it, in her desperation to find him, she was feeling a little sick and her head was thumping, she knew she had to pull herself together for the sake of Joe and the children.

Joe! Oh my god…Joe, she had rushed out of the factory and over to the school without even a thought of Joe, oh good heavens, what was she thinking about? She must find Joe and get back to the girls. As she ran back to the school her mind kept flashing back to that dirty little face, she was sure it had belonged to Harry.

By now she was crying quite freely and muttering out loud.."Joe..Oh ..Joe..Harry's alive, I know he is, where is Peggy?" She felt two arms around her and a voice saying softly; "It's alright mum we are all safe, don't worry, Dad is at the first aid post helping with the casualties, and Harry too. Mrs. Phipps has taken charge of Hilda and Betty". Peggy held her mum tightly until her sobbing subsided then they both walked over to the first aid post, holding hands tightly trying to soothe each others nerves.

The ambulances had arrived and were already transporting the injured children to the hospital. The ambulance men worked silently and methodically getting the children, who were still alive away first. Nine little bodies lay still and silent covered with a blanket from head to toe, it was such a tragedy. It was hard to take in, that those nine little bodies would never laugh or play again. Why was life so cruel at times, thought Sal to herself; just innocent babes.

There was nothing else the Cheadle family could do now the professionals had taken over. Joe took them home, all were very tired and upset, it was a day they would never forget, no matter how hard they were to try.

When they arrived home Sal made them all sit down while she made a hot cup of tea, with plenty of sugar in it.

After the children had been in bed for an hour, Sal crept up the stairs to make sure they were alright. Hilda and Betty were fast asleep; she thought Harry was as well, until she heard a faint sobbing noise as she was going down the stairs. She stood listening for a few seconds while wondering what to do, should she go to him; or let him cry it out of his system. He was such a tough little fellow, but after chewing it over with herself, she decided to go to him. He was really tearing at her heartstrings.

Sal opened the door a little and whispered "May I come in Harry?" he sat up quickly brushing his tears away with the back of his hand, trying to pretend he was all right.

As Sal bent over him, he suddenly threw his arms around her neck and in between sobs he said; "That poor little girl mum…she was dead, and still holding the…. the boys hand….bloody war!"

Sal held him close saying soothingly, "There …there Harry, you mustn't fret so and although I agree with what you say; you shouldn't swear, but she smiled at him and whispered "Bloody war"

When she came down the stairs Joe was sitting in front of the fire listening to the wireless, he looked up, "Everything okay Sal?"

She looked thoughtful, "You know Joe it's a funny thing but both Harry and Betty have called me mum today, in fact I think Betty called me mummy." The children usually called her Aunt Sally.

Joe looked at her tenderly and said, "It's funny how your mind works under stress, but don't worry dear, they won't forget their real mother, although she hasn't kept in touch with them much has she?"

Chapter Nine

Until the school had been made safe and the infant's part rebuilt, the children did there schooling in different churches and available halls, according to their ages. Luckily Betty and Hilda went to the same church for most of their lessons. Peggy and Harry were on their own.

Peggy left school at Easter and went to work in an office, until she was old enough to join the wrens. At first she didn't like office work but after about six months, she had become very friendly with two other girls. They were in the same building as Peggy, but in a different office. Peggy had been assigned to the wages department and was enjoying it much better and hoped one-day to become the directors secretary. She wasn't quite so sure about going in the wrens anymore.

Peggy found the director a very dishy fellow, although she had had no experience of men, as yet, she would fantasise about him. He was quite young for a man in his position, she thought to herself. I wonder what it would be like to be kissed by him, his lips looked soft and tender, his blue eyes like cool waters running deep.

She was brought out of her daydream by a shrill ringing, she realised it was the phone and in a dreamy voice answered it. Luckily it was one of the girls from another office and not an important client.

Molly and June both worked in the sales office, but they met Peggy in the canteen for their breaks. If it was only a drink they wanted they would go to the staff room, where it was quieter and they could about boys without being overheard. The staff room had adequate facilities for coffee and tea making.

Molly and June were both a little older than Peggy was and much more experienced on the subject of men. Peggy thought she could learn a lot listening to them both.

"We are going to the camp dance on Saturday Peg, why don't you come with us?"

"But I can't dance," poor Peggy looked so embarrassed, the other two girls started to laugh; "Don't worry about that, you will soon learn to jive and jitterbug, the Yanks are good teachers."

Peggy hung her head, and mumbled, "I don't think mum will let me go to an American camp.

"Don't tell her then," said June, "tell her you are coming to my birthday party and will be late home

"But it's not your birthday, that would be telling lies

June looked at her crossly, "Don't be silly, your mum doesn't even know me, let alone know when my birthday is."

"Hey look at the time," shouted Molly, "we had better get back to work before we get the sack."

Friday night Peggy approached her mother and asked

if she could go to a birthday party. Sal was quite pleased, as she had heard so much about Peggy's friends at work; she felt she already knew them.

Sal smiled at her daughter, "You ought to get out a bit now dear, you are nearly seventeen and quite sensible. I'm sure you know how to behave yourself. What time will you be home?"

"Well that's the trouble mum, I'm afraid it will be quite late, but June said I could stay at her house,..Erm.. that's if you don't mind." Peggy felt so guilty lying to her mother like this, and she felt sick. She had never lied in her life especially to her mother. She wasn't happy about it at all.

Saturday morning Peggy washed her hair in preparation for the dance. She had lovely hair, long and wavy and when it had just been washed it shone like silk She had developed into a very attractive young lady, long shapely legs and a very curvy but slender body. Her big blue eyes went very well with her naturally blonde hair and fair complexion. Joe thought her a real smasher.

Peggy wore her hair in a ponytail whilst she was at work, but when she let it hang loose she looked a little more mature and very feminine. Sal sighed when she saw her daughter dressed ready to go; she looked so beautiful, yet innocent to the extreme. Sal felt so proud of her, she wanted to sweep her up into her arms and hug her. She thought to herself…My daughter.

Peggy had chosen to wear a white outfit, that her mother had made for her, it was a very full dirndle skirt edged with coloured braiding, with a square neck blouse to match; it was ideal for jiving and such.

Joe had gone to the local for a drink with his mate; it was very rare that Joe went out without Sal. She thought it would be a nice change for him and do him good; besides she had some ironing she wanted to get on with.

Sal loved to sing when she was doing any kind of housework; especially if she thought she was on her own She had a lovely voice and could reach all the high notes with perfection.

"Little sir echo how do you do..Hello"

"Ello ow do you do,"

Sal laughed, "Oh hello Harry I thought you were playing in the yard, I didn't hear you come in"

"I came in as soon as I heard you singing Aunt Sally, I knew then you must be on your own.

"I see you have come to keep me company have you?" Harry looked so serious, she knew something was bothering him.

"If you ain't too busy Aunt Sally, can we sit and have a chat, just the two of us like,"

"Yes of course darling, that would be nice. Let me just pack the ironing away, then we can sit in the front room, it's more comfortable in there."

This was unusual for Harry, most of the time he loved to play outside in the yard with the football Joe had bought him.

When they were comfortably settled by the fire Sal looked at him enquiringly, and when he hung his head, she realised he was crying softly to himself. Sal went over and knelt beside him; "What is the matter Harry? Are you unhappy here?"

Before she could say anymore he flung his arms around her neck and sobbed; "I want you to be my mum as well as Peggy's."

"But what about you're own mum and dad? How do you think they would feel?" Sals heart went out to him and she wanted nothing better herself. She knew she had to be very careful how she handled the situation.

"I 'ates me dad, and me mum is afraid on him erself; she never sticks up for me when he belts me."

Sal noticed he had reverted back to his own slang, just as she thought he was speaking better of late. But just at this moment in time it didn't seem very important, so she didn't attempt to correct him

"If I come to church with you tomorrow, do you think God would listen to somebody like me?"

Sal hugged him closer to her, "I am sure he would

Harry; he is a very understanding person"

That night when the children were in bed asleep, Sal told Joe about the conversation she had had with harry. They were so engrossed in their discussion they hadn't really noticed the time. "Do you realise old lady it is almost half past twelve?"

Joe was just about to lock the front door, when he thought he heard a noise outside, he peeped his head out of the door and got the shock of his life. Who should be out there, but Peggy; looking very dishevelled, and tears streaming down her face.

"Good heavens child, what on earth is going on? We thought you were staying at your friends house" he led her inside and softly called Sal. He didn't want to wake the other children.

Peggy flopped wearily in a chair sobbing; "Oh mum, I am so sorry, I'm afraid I lied to you; I was not going to a birthday party at all, she hesitated, we went to a dance at the American camp."

Sal was so stunned, at first she could find nothing to say. It was Joe who spoke first, "Then why, em, how come your clothes are in such a state? And where are your friends now?"

"It was so awful" she sobbed, "The dance was fine, but afterwards three yanks wanted us to go to their billets with them. I said no but the other two went. The yank I was supposed to be with, started to undo the zip on my skirt, and pulled up my blouse. He was so strong I had to bite his hand to make him let go of me; then I just ran and ran".

Sal was feeling cross that Peggy had felt it necessary to lie to her about the party, being so deceitful was not at all like her Peggy. Sal was always so sure she could trust all of her children. Now she wasn't so sure.

"We will discuss this further in the morning," said Joe, "but for now I think we could all do with some sleep."

Joe and Sal undressed in silence, they were both feeling depressed, what with the situation with Harry and now Peggy.

"What are we going to do Joe?" Sal sighed heavily.

"Get some sleep darling if possible, and talk things over in the morning, or rather later this morning."

Sal lay awake for most of the night, going over in her mind all that had happened. By the time she managed to drift off, Joe was waking her up with a hot cup of tea.

"I guess you could do with this my darling, I know you didn't get much sleep." He handed her the cup and saucer, which she took gratefully.

When Sal arrived downstairs Peggy was already in the kitchen, as if she had been waiting for her mother.

"Well young lady, I think we will have our breakfast first, then we can have a talk in the front room in peace and quiet."

They sat at the table in silence, neither eating very much. Joe said nothing to either of them; he just quietly tucked into his breakfast, trying to look as if he was enjoying it.

"I will clear away and wash up the breakfast things Sal, while you and Peggy have a talk, come on Harry you and the girls can give me a hand. We'll leave the women to it," he winked at Sal as he spoke.

He was always so understanding was Joe; this was one of his many qualities Sal had fallen in love with, all those years ago.

As they sat in the easy chairs, Sal turned to her daughter, she looked so upset and nervous, and Sal's heart went out to her as she spoke in a soft voice, "I think Peggy it would be best if you explain by starting from the beginning.

Sal listened to her daughters story and soon realised it had been quite a daunting experience for her, she also knew it wouldn't be repeated.

"Well dear, I'm sure you know how foolish you have been without me telling you. I must say though how disappointed I am that you felt the need to lie to me, I find that very hurtful as your dad and I have always tried to be fair, however we will let the matter drop now as I am sure your experience was punishment enough."

Peggy went to her mother and put her arms around her saying, "I can promise you now mum it will never happen again;..I do love you mum"

Sal returned to the kitchen to find Joe and Harry had finished clearing up and were out in the yard playing their own game of cricket. She stood and watched from the window, they looked so happy together, she wondered if he was filling the gap in Joe's life that Georgie had left.

They must have sensed her watching them, for they both looked up at the window at the same time, and both waved.

Harry looked so happy, she thought she wouldn't mention his parents, she would wait until he brought the subject up again himself, she knew she was only playing for time.

Chapter Ten

Sunday morning! Sal could not believe her eyes, when Harry came down the stairs, all dressed up in his Sunday best clothes, his hair neatly combed.

"Will I do Aunt Sally? I'm already for church"

Sal smiled, so he hadn't forgotten after all, "you look very smart dear, I am very proud of you"

Hilda and Betty attended the Sunday school, Peggy usually took them as she helped the Sunday school teacher take the lessons, she enjoyed reading little bible stories out loud to the children.

Sal was quite surprised when she heard Harry singing out with gusto, "All things bright and bootiful" she almost laughed, but remembered where she was. She was surprised he even knew the words, so forgave him his pronunciation.

During the prayers Sal could hear a little murmur and felt sure she heard the words 'please God' it was then she knew it was Harry praying to God to become permanently a member of her family. She was silently praying herself for guidance on the subject; she hadn't got the right to say yes to him; as much as she dearly would have liked. Sal at this point made up her mind she would go and see the welfare as soon as it was convenient. But what about the two little girls, she wouldn't want to split the family up, but surely the mother wouldn't let them go. 'Oh dear what a mess', She loved all three of them as if they were already her own, but Harry had a special place in her heart, bless him he had had such a lot to bear in his young life.

Wednesday lunchtime Sal had just reached the front door when she had such a strange feeling, it was like cold fingers running up and down her spine. She visibly shivered as she entered the house feeling very uneasy.

She only had time to put the kettle on, when there was a knock at the door, it made Sal jump, nobody called to see her in her lunch break, she only had half an hour, just enough time to peel the vegetables for their dinner and have a quick cup of tea. She felt afraid,..of what!... she didn't know, but she had a strong feeling something was wrong. Her mind went to Fred, "please God NO" she almost shouted out loud.

When she opened the door and saw Mrs.Polter standing there, a different kind of fear overtook her; had she come to take the children away, back to their proper parents? Mrs Polters face looked very serious and she looked most uncomfortable.

"May I come in Mrs. Cheadle? I'm afraid I have some very sad news, especially for the children".

"Please come into the front room and sit down, I'm afraid the children are at school"

"Yes I realise that, that is why I have come early, I knew you came home in your lunch break. I wanted to talk to you before I tell the children."

"Look I have just made a pot of tea, would you like one? You look as if you could do with one;"she smiled kindly, as she could see Mrs. Polter was very nervous and on edge. When they were both settled in a chair with a cup of tea, Mrs. Polter began to explain the reason for her visit.

"I am afraid last night there was a particularly bad raid on London, the children's parents were out at the public house when a bomb fell, it was a direct hit on the building and I'm afraid that no one survived."

Sal sat very still as if mesmerised, her face had turned grey, she wanted to say something, but the words just wouldn't come out of her mouth, her mind was saying over and over ..Poor Betty... Poor Hilda, but strangely not poor Harry!

When the children arrived home from school, they were chattering and laughing, quite unaware of the tragedy that had befell them.

"Hello" said Hilda politely to Mrs Polter, "Have you come to fetch us home?" Mrs Polter and Sal looked at one another awkwardly

"I think you had better come and sit down quietly children Mrs. Polter has something to tell you," With this Sal picked betty up and sat her on her lap, inviting Hilda to sit in the same armchair beside her, it was a tight squeeze, but Sal felt she had to have them close to her. Harry plonked himself on the floor at Sal's feet, resting his arms on her knee. He often sat like this in the evenings, when she would read them a story before going to bed.

The two girls acted as was natural and expected, but neither Sal nor Mrs. Polter was prepared for Harry's reaction, they were both taken by complete surprise.

Poor Harry,..he laughed hysterically at first, then with tears streaming down his sad little face, he stuttered;"I'm s s sorry she's dead.. but I ent s sorry o'er im…ees dead ….eas dead..I'm glad"

His voice was getting louder and louder, almost to screaming pitch. Sal quickly took charge of him and left the girls in the capable hands of Mrs. Polter.

Harry put his arms round Sals neck as she picked him up; he clung so tightly she could hardly breath. Her own face was wet with tears as she rocked and comforted him.

Joe and Peggy arrived home at the same time and were both devastated when told the news. Joe took hold of Harry and without thinking said; "Come on son, let's go for a walk" Harry cottoned on to Joe's words, he had called him Son!

"Can I really be your son now?" he asked tearfully "Can I call you mum and dad like Peggy does?" he sounded so excited, Joe couldn't speak he could only glance helplessly at Sal.

Mrs. Polter said rather stiffly, "I think both you and Mr Cheadle had better come to my office tomorrow morning Mrs. Cheadle, we have a lot to discuss, but in the meantime I would advise you not to raise any false hopes." She sounded firm without being too unkind.

"Goodbye Mrs. Polter, I shan't make a stupid mistake like that again in a hurry, I can assure you we will both be very careful in future; please accept my apologies." With this Joe went to the door and shook hands with her as she left.

When Joe came back in the room, he did not say a word, he just put his jacket on and led Harry, (who was ready and waiting), outside.

Peggy helped her mother with the two girls, and to get the dinner ready, between them they just about coped, but only just; it had been such a trauma, Sal felt drained and exhausted.

It was three months before the authorities gave Sal and Joe the go ahead to apply for the adoption of Harry, Hilda and Betty. By then the children had got over their initial grief and were almost back to normal. Betty hadn't wet the bed for the last three nights now. It's strange how a tragedy can upset your whole system. Harry appeared not to care but Sal knew he was hurting a little inside for his mother. He had loved her in spite of her weakness for not standing up to her husband. The poor lamb, Harry had such an old head; for such young shoulders.

Chapter Eleven

Sal was feeling very tired these days, she was more than a little worried as she had missed two periods now. She was afraid to go to the doctor in case he told her she was pregnant. She had not so far had any morning sickness, which made her wonder, as she had suffered dreadfully that way with her other pregnancies. She knew she would have to do something about it soon though. Luckily Joe had been kept too busy at work to keep track of dates; he had been so tired of late he had been falling asleep as soon as his head touched the pillow.

Tuesday afternoon Sal was feeling so exhausted at work that she had to come home. She had made up her mind to go to the doctors that evening, if she went early enough she could be back home again before Joe, it all depended how many were in the waiting room before her.

When she arrived at the surgery, there was only six people waiting and luckily they didn't all want to see Dr. Cozen.

Sal tapped gently on the door before entering the doctor's room, he looked quite surprised to see her at first, but Sal soon realised it was because she looked so peaky and troubled!

"Hello Mrs. Cheadle and what can I do for you? Please take a seat."   Sal told him how she was feeling and what she feared. He sat and listened as if he was analysing every word she spoke.

"Well I think the first thing is to examine you, if you would just get undressed and lie on the couch"

He gave her an internal examination and assured her she was not pregnant. "You won't like it very much my dear, but it looks like you are in the early stages of the change. I am going to give you a tonic and some tablets, to help ease the burden of it. I would like a blood test and a urine specimen before you go home. Do you think you could oblige me my dear? he smiled. Sal had never noticed before what big brown eyes he'd got; you seemed to notice his eyebrows first, as they were very bushy, with a hint of grey. He had always been kind to her and her family and was very upset himself when they had lost Georgie.

Sal went home feeling a little easier in her mind, although she was a little surprised to find she felt a slight disappointment. However now she could tell Joe and they could have a laugh about it ..(In the change indeed!)

When Sal opened the front door, there on the mat, lay a letter; she knew at once it was from Fred. She opened it with a feeling of excitement and almost shouted out loud when she read it. Fred was coming home on leave for ten whole days! She could hardly compose herself as she prepared the evening meal.

Hilda and Betty were the first to arrive home, they went out to play in the back yard with their dolls and prams, which Sal and Joe had bought them for their birthdays. They had both been so thrilled , they had never had anything like this before.

Harry arrived home soon after looking dirty and bedraggled. The sleeve of his shirt was torn and he had a little blood on his upper lip.

Sal looked at him crossly; "Have you been fighting again Harry?…Why can't you stay out of trouble?"

Harry looked at her sheepishly, "Aw I'm sorry mum, but Tommy Black was saying things about our Peggy, so I thumped him; then we had a proper fight, you know fisty cuffs. I made his nose bleed ever so bad, and cut his lip an all"

"Alright.. alright Harry, that's enough about the fight, but I would like to hear what he was saying about Peggy to make you fight over it"

Sal waited a few seconds for an answer, but it was pretty obvious Harry didn't want to say. "Now look here young man" Sal tried to sound cross, "We don't have any secrets in this house, and as you are now one of the family I expect you to tell me what is being said about your sister to cause a fight"

Harry hung his head and mumbled, "He said things", and here he hesitated. "Well I'm listening Harry but I don't hear anything," she realised it was difficult for him, but she had to know what was being said about her daughter.

"He said our Peg went with 'Yanks' and did things" here he hesitated again, Sal looked at him enquiringly, "You know mum, sex and ...and stuff like that" If Sal had not felt so angry, she would have laughed at the expression on Harry's face.

Mrs. Black worked at the factory, in the same room as Sal, so she made up her mind to have a chat with her in the morning during their tea break, and see if she could sort things out. Sal wasn't going to have her children's name blackened; not if she could help it. Her Peggy was a good girl, she wouldn't do anything like that, or would she?...she had lied to her....No...No...that was different, her Peggy wasn't that sort of girl.

With all this upset going on she had almost forgotten the letter, she sent Harry upstairs to wash and change his shirt, while she carried on getting the evening meal ready.

When they were all sitting down to eat, Sal took the letter out of her apron pocket and handed it to Joe. The contents brought a broad grin to his face, "Well that's the best news we've had in months"

Harry looked puzzled, "Have our final adoption papers come through dad?.. Can I see them? Have we got a new birth certificate, with our new name on, Harry Cheadle" he said proudly

Joe looked a little uncomfortable, "no son, not yet, but this news is almost as good" he winked at Sal as he spoke, and she nodded her approval as she said, "You haven't met our eldest boy yet children have you? The one we told you was in the army,..well he is coming home on leave for ten whole days"

"Cor that's the one that's a blacksmith aint it mum?" Harry sounded excited. Sal knew they would all like her Fred! She smiled at Harry; in fact it was more of a broad grin than a smile.

The rest of the evening was spent with the children asking questions about Fred and playing card games. They loved a game of 'snap' especially when mum joined in.

Chapter Twelve

After the children were settled down for the night, Sal and Joe sat down each side of the fireplace to talk over the day's events.

"Would you have really minded darling if you had of been pregnant?" Joe asked in a tender voice.

"No not really dear, although I think we have enough to cope with, with Harry just now" They both laughed. "Yes Harry! I wonder what Fred will make of him"

As they lay in each other's arms that night, Sal felt more relaxed than she had felt for months. Joe's lovemaking had a tenderness she hadn't felt before. Her whole body responded to his gentle caresses, filling her with a passion and longing. Their hearts and bodies were fulfilled, their emotions and excitement taking them to the final crescendo. Exhausted they lay still, as if joined, listening to the rhythm of their own hearts. Before she finally fell asleep, Sal whispered in her husband's ear " In the change indeed"

The day arrived for Fred's homecoming, Sal had cleaned the house from top to bottom, the children were bathed and dressed in their Sunday best. Joe laughed and said, "Darling It's Fred coming not the King, he wouldn't want you to go to all this trouble"

She had prepared Fred's favourite meal and had got herself in such a state of excitement. It seemed forever and a day since they had seen their Fred.

At first Hilda and Betty were very shy with Fred, but Harry, he sparked off a friendship that was unbelievable. Sal and Joe were happy with their lot.

The first thing Fred wanted to do the next morning, was to go to the forge to see Sam. "Coming with me Harry?" He didn't need asking twice; he was more than ready to go with Fred.

Sam was so pleased to see Fred home he almost shed a few tears. "This calls for a celebration lad, let's go down the pub for a pint. We can sit in the garden so the boy can come with us"

"My names Harry, can I have a pint as well?" "No you can't" laughed Fred, clipping him playfully across the ear, "It will be a lemonade and a packet of crisps or nothing" He ruffled Harry's hair, "You're a cheeky beggar aren't you?"

There was so much fun and frivolity; the week seemed over before it began. Sal couldn't believe it was nearly all over, and she would be losing her son again. Joe tried to comfort her, "He will be home again soon lass, and hopefully the war won't last forever."

The evening before Fred's return to his unit, he took Harry for a walk. They sat on a style that led to the bridle walk and talked.

As Harry talked, Fred could almost see the face of the man Harry had once known as dad. He could feel the pain of the beatings this young boy had endured. Harry was so explicit with his description; it was as if he was re-living it. Fred couldn't bear the pain in this young lads eyes, he hugged him close and whispered, "It's alright lad, you are one of us now, one big happy family, after the war is over how would you like to work at the forge with me and Sam? I'm sure there would be room for you"

Harry was silent for a few minutes before he said soberly, and with conviction; "I don't want to offend you Fred, but I really do want to be a doctor. Ever since I saw that little girl and boy clutching each others hands, you know the one I told you about in that bloody air-raid"

"Well I think that's very commendable of you Harry, but if you really want to be a doctor, you will have to learn to talk properly, instead of all that slang you come out with. No…No".. here Fred put his hand out as Harry jumped ready to go in a huff. "I don't mean you have to talk posh and la-de-da, but you do have to have a good bedside manner"

"I haven't told mum yet Fred, but I think she might have a good idea, as I keep getting told off, Cause I keep putting bandage on next doors dogs legs."

Fred roared with laughter, he could just imagine this little lad trying to put a bandage on the big Alsatian dogs legs. It was just as well he was a placid dog and knew Harry well.

"Come on you toad," Fred laughed, "let's get off home, mum will wonder where we've got to. I would like to be at home with just the family tonight, as I have to leave in the morning"

"Race you home," shouted Harry sprinting off. They arrived back at the house, exhausted...Out of breath... but happy....oh yes ...very happy.

The evening went very quickly, lots of laughter and chatter, but Joe knew deep down Sal was brooding at the thought of Fred going away again.

The only thing that had spoilt it all was the fact that Mary couldn't get away from collage. It seemed such a long time since her family had been complete. She was glad Peggy had changed her mind about going in the wrens, she appeared to be getting on very well at the office where she worked. Although she didn't go dancing with her two friends anymore, they still had their dinner breaks together. They told Peggy all sorts of stories about what they got up to, she could quite understand her mothers concern for her. Sal used to say 'As sure as eggs are eggs those two will be in trouble before they reach twenty'

Next morning brought chaos, everyone getting in each other's way. There was much noise and confusion, they almost missed the big brown envelope that came hurtling through the letterbox and landed on the doormat.

Sal picked it up and knew at once it was the final papers for the children's adoption. They were finally her family now, how excited they would be when she told them. It would help to soften the blow of Fred's departure, and when it was time to go, Harry shook Fred's hand and said in a grown up voice, "So long Brother, take care of yourself"

To which Fred replied, "So long Doctor Cheadle",

and winked cheekily at him. Harry pulled himself up to his fullest height and grinned from ear to ear. Sal could have sworn he grew ten inches, and ten years older, he looked so proud.

Joe put his arm round Sal's waist and said, "He'll be home again soon darling, and when this war is finally over we will have a big party for him..For them all"… ."Yes darling for them all" she replied..

"In the meantime Sal, do you think we ought to do something special to celebrate, and welcome the children into our family."

"I know Joe, how about if we take them to the Zoo on Sunday. I will make up a picnic basket, so it won't cost too much, I'm sure the girls would like it"

Joe laughed, "I wonder what Harry will make of the monkeys, or more to the point, what will they make of Harry!" They both laughed and hugged each other. "Come on Let's go and put it to them" said Joe.

All three of them were excited, as they had never been

to a Zoo before. Hilda looked quite alarmed as she said "they won't bite us or eat us up will they mummy" "No darling" said Sal giving her a big cuddle. "They are all in big cages and you see them through the bars, everything is safe dear, besides we girls will have Joe and Harry to look after us won't we?" This seemed to satisfy both the girls.

Sunday turned out to be a very warm day, the sun was shining and not a cloud in the sky. Sal made the sandwiches and made a few fairy cakes ready for the picnic. Harry was hopping about getting in everyone's way in his excitement. In the end Sal sent him upstairs to have a wash and get ready, it was the only way she could get him from under her feet.

When they were almost ready to go, Sal called out to Harry to come downstairs. They couldn't believe their eyes when Harry started to walk casually down, he was wearing a pair of Fred's long trousers, although he was quite tall for his age, they were still too big and were all concertina down the bottom of each leg. Sal stood with her mouth open wide, in amazement, then she burst out laughing "Harry we haven't time for games, that is if you want to catch the bus for the Zoo"

"I'm not playing games mum, Fred said I could borrow them if I liked, besides who ever heard of a doctor wearing short pants?"

"Yes dear, who ever did" she answered kindly, but I think for today you had better put your short ones on and we will see about getting you some new ones" That seemed to satisfy him and he made haste to change.

Luckily for them the bus was a little late, so they just caught it in time. Hilda kept close to Sal, she seemed a little nervous today; Her small hands were quite clammy as she held on tight to Sal's. I hope she isn't sickening for anything she thought to herself.

All three children were thrilled at the antics of the monkeys and enjoyed a ride on the elephant; especially Harry, Betty and Hilda was a little scared at first. They all enjoyed the picnic, which was followed by an ice cream each.

When they at last arrived home again they were all tired and Betty and Hilda were quite ready for bed, Sal kissed them both as she tucked them in "Goodnight my darlings" They both responded with a very sleepy 'night night.'

Harry was allowed to stay up a little later than the girls, as he was a little older. Her and Joe played a couple of games of cards with him before he went up to bed.

"No messing about Harry, I will be up to say goodnight in five minutes" She made a point of seeing them all safely tucked in and giving them a goodnight kiss. As she was tucking Harry in he said, "Mum did you mean it about me having some new trousers? If so, do you think I could have long ones now, after all I'm nearly thirteen now? I shall be leaving school next year"

"Of course dear I meant every word I said. But if you are going to be a doctor you won't be leaving school exactly will you?"

She discussed things with Joe, "Do you think he will ever be a doctor dear, he does seem to have made up his mind, I thought at first he would grow out of the idea, but I'm afraid I was wrong."

"We will have to wait and see Sal, only time will tell, I don't think he will ever forget that day at the school, it made a real impact on him"

There seemed to be no end to this blessed war, things were getting more and more difficult as each week passed. Sal hated having to queue for everything, and watching every coupon, with the rationing, it felt as if it would never end. Sal realised she was luckier than a good many, she still had her Joe and most of her children around her. Poor Mrs. Brown had lost two of her sons within a week of each other; they were both on the same ship that had been torpedoed. When they found and picked them up, Jim was still alive; but so badly injured he died without gaining consciousness. Sal didn't know what she would do if she lost her Fred.

Mary was home from collage at last, and now she was qualified, she had landed herself a good job, teaching in the infant's school close by. Sal wished she lived at home though instead of sharing a flat with two other young girls, they had all three qualified at the same time.

Sal came home from work Tuesday lunch time as she hadn't felt like eating sandwiches at work, it must have been an Oman for no sooner had she made a cup of tea, than there was a knock on the door. She felt a little panic button had been pressed, and when she opened the door, there stood a young lad with a telegram in his hand. Sal felt her whole body shake with fear; it could only be one thing! She looked at the lad as she held out her shaking hand to take the piece of paper. "I'm sorry Mrs," he said in a soft voice, for he knew what it meant, he had delivered so many in his short life. Sal just held it as she shut the door; she didn't seem to have the strength to open it. She should be getting back to work; she had had more than an hour off, instead of the half-hour allowed.

The front door opened and in walked Joe, he looked at her enquiringly but she looked in a daze.

"What's the matter darling? Why aren't you at work?" It was then he saw the unopened telegram in her hand.

He gently took it from her; (it read) I am sorry to inform you your son is missing. believed killed.

Joe almost fell to the floor he was that stunned, no wonder Sal hadn't come back to work He held her close, not knowing what to say, they were both hurting and the tears flowed freely. Time went by without them even realising it, until a small hand crept silently in each of theirs. They looked up together, both startled out of their grief; "Harry" they hadn't heard him come in and didn't realise the time. They showed him the telegram and without a word, he solemnly walked out of the room and went upstairs.

Joe gave him a few minutes on his own, he knew he would be fretting. They decided not to tell Hilda and Betty, they were too young to feel the burden of war, let them grow up a little first, reality of tragedy and life would be on them soon enough. Harry had taken it very badly; Joe had a problem trying to console him,"Why my brother?... Why?... I've only just found him" he sobbed in Joe's arms."Sh, Sh son, life can be very cruel, we have to try and be brave after all the telegram said missing didn't it? So they don't know for certain he is" Joe couldn't bring out the last word, he just hugged Harry tighter, "let's hope and pray they find him and that he is alive. I will have to go and see to your mum now; you can imagine what sort of state she is in."

He left Harry still quietly sobbing, and found Sal in the front room polishing the furniture vigorously. "Darling, what are you doing? Come on, come with me, let's go for a walk down the lane, It will help to clear our heads so we can cope with everyday things. Come on dear"

She put her duster down on the table, she was in a daze and doing as she was told as if she was a child. Joe took her hand and together they walked down the lane. There was no need for words; they both knew how the other was feeling.

They sat on an old tree trunk, it had always been there favourite spot, but they hadn't been here for years now. "Do you remember how we used to come here Sal, long before we moved into Grundy Street?"

"Yes darling I remember" she answered softly, "So much has happened in our lives, and yet now it seems like only yesterday we sat here, holding hands and planning for our future "

Sal jumped up, "Peggy! ...Oh Joe, we haven't told Peggy yet or Mary, I do hope Harry doesn't say anything to them. Peggy should be home by now." They hurried as fast as they could; Sal almost had to trot to keep up with Joe. When they arrived home Harry was still in his room; they both gave a sigh of relief. Sal noticed the telegram had gone; "Oh Joe what do you think has happened to it?" A small voice came from upstairs, it was Harry!

"I've got it mum in case Hilda and Betty saw it, I didn't think you would want them to read it" Joe was so proud to think Harry could act so responsibly and grown up, he really had matured in the last few weeks, NO! He matured after the school was bombed, that is when he started to change.

Joe would do everything in his power to help Harry become a doctor, after all he deserved it, and they had noticed his schoolwork had improved dramatically. His behaviour had improved two; why hadn't he noticed it before?

Peggy and Mary were devastated when they were told about their brother. There was nothing Sal or Joe could do to lesson the pain for them, they could only hold them close and let them weep.

Chapter Thirteen

Peggy came home from work full of excitement; a young man from the offices where she worked had asked her to join a voluntary service with him. They would work for the Red Cross, but within the hospital. Sal wasn't sure if it was the work, or the fact of the lad asking her, that had caused the slight flush on her cheeks. "I thought mum once I had got established there I could ask Harry if he would like to help, it would give him a little insight into hospital procedure wouldn't it?"

Sal hesitated, "Erm yes I suppose it would, that would be nice dear." It was too early to say anything to Harry just yet, they would wait and see how Peggy got on.

"What is the lad's name Peggy? You haven't mentioned him before."

Peggy blushed even more," Well to tell you the truth mum, I've had my eye on him for quite sometime now" she giggled. "But I didn't think he had ever noticed me. You will like him mum, he's got very dark hair and big brown eyes, a long straight nose and full smiling lips" she sounded so dreamy.

Sal couldn't help smiling, as Peggy seemed to be in a trance as she spoke about him. He must be really something, she thought, for Peggy to be so smitten. "Our first day at the hospital is next Saturday, but Pete said he would like to take me to the pictures on Friday night." She looked anxiously at her mother, "Do you think I should go?" she asked.

"Darling only you can answer that, you are old enough now to know if you like him well enough to say yes. After all he isn't asking you to do anything wrong is he?"

"Good heavens mum no", she sounded shocked," I think we have got our wires crossed Peggy I didn't mean what you thought" They both burst out laughing,"We are a pair," said Sal.

Peggy rushed home from work on Friday, as she wanted to wash her hair, she wanted to look her best for Pete. She didn't stop to eat any dinner. "Pete and I will get a bag of chips on the way home mum"

When she was ready and waiting for Pete to call, Sal looked at her and said, "My Peggy, you look lovely," Out of the blue Harry said, "If I was a bit older I would take you out myself." They all laughed, but Sal suspected Harry had meant it and she felt a little worried, after all they were not blood relations were they. She gave her head a mental shake, to get the thought right out of it.

Pete had been courting Peggy for sometime now and it was turning into a meaningful relationship. Joe joked and said he could even hear the wedding bells.

Peggy was still writing to Bill, they had become very good friends, but both new that's all it was friendship. It had been two months now since she had heard from him, she hoped nothing had happened to him like their Fred.

A letter arrived on Tuesday morning; it was for Peggy, from the hospital. She had been asked if she would like to visit the military hospital up north. Transport would be laid on and a meal provided, as they would be spending the whole day there She had two days to make her mind up so they could offer the place to someone else if necessary. When she spoke to Pete about it next day, he was delighted as he had also had a letter. They both replied and accepted without delay.

Sal was a little bit apprehensive about it; it seemed a long way to go; what if there was an air raid! Both Peggy and Pete assured her it would be okay, they would both be safe, after all it looked as if the war would end soon. There was a lot of talk about it coming to an end.

That night in bed her and Joe discussed the situation, Joe was quite confident about the war ending. He held Sal lovingly in his arms, kissing her passionately, and whispering in her ear, "Let's not think about it just now darling, at this moment I need you,…I love you so much"…Sal relaxed and enjoyed.

Tuesday morning Peggy was already and waiting for her transport ten minutes early. Sal was fussing over her like a mother hen. Peggy laughed, "For goodness sake mother you will be clucking like a hen next"

When the taxi arrived, Pete was already sitting in it with a big grin on his face. Sal smiled and waved them off, she was still feeling a little nervous about it.

She gave herself a mental shake, she really had to stop this silliness and get the children ready for school. Hilda looked a little pale and said she had a head ache Sal thought she looked a little flushed and when she examined her, her body was covered in spots. "Oh dear darling, I think you may have the measles, you will have to stay in bed and I will ask Doctor Cozen to come in and see you"

Poor Hilda started to cry, "What are you crying for darling, it isn't anything serious, the doctor will soon make you better"

"Mrs. Jones Tommy, he died from the measles" she sobbed. "Well that's because he didn't have Dr. Cozen to look after him," she said soothingly.

Sal stroked her hand over Hilda's hair and in less than five minutes she was fast asleep. Doctor Cozen told Sal to keep Betty off school. He didn't want her to spread any germs, anything to avoid an epidemic. Measles was one of the worst child illnesses, it could lead to blindness, deafness or even be fatal. It was more than likely Betty would go down with it next.

Harry came home from school and almost collapsed on the sofa, Sal knew at once he must have caught the measles off Hilda, they had all thought it would be Betty.

Sal certainly had her work cut out with two of them being ill, Joe had told her to stay at home and nurse the children, never mind the factory, they could manage without her until the children were better.

After three weeks of nursing the children Sal started to look peaky herself. Joe was quite worried he hoped Sal wasn't going to go down with the measles as well. Hilda and Betty were back at school but Harry was still listless and very pale. Dr. Cozen gave him a good tonic; he thought some of it was down to the fact that he was growing at a rapid rate now. He was almost as tall as Joe was, but still very slim. He was growing into a good-looking lad, and would have no trouble finding a nice girl friend when the time was right.

Chapter Fourteen

Peggy and Pete arrived at the Military Hospital In the middle of the morning; it had been a long and uneventful journey. The Matron and an official from the Red Cross greeted them.

"I think you would probably appreciate a nice hot cup of tea after your long journey, then we will give you a tour around the hospital"

Both Peggy and Pete were grateful for a cup of tea; Peggy was feeling a little sick after such a long ride. She wasn't used to cars, especially long rides like that, and in the back of the vehicle too. When they had finished their tea and biscuits, they were escorted onto the wards.

Some of the wards were quite large and airy,

everywhere was clean and fresh, the male patients cheerful and talkative. Peggy learned quite a lot about some of them; they all seemed willing to talk about their experiences. Pete suspected some of the tales they told, were not strictly true, they were just making light of everything. One poor sailor had his arm in plaster and was one leg missing, he laughed at Peggy and said, "the poor bloody whales looked hungry so I threw them a meal." Peggy tried to laugh but she felt more like crying.

Matron took them both for a meal at dinnertime; they had it in the hospital canteen. They met a lot of the nursing staff there, and were able to ask many questions. "My young brother would love to have been here today, he want's to be a doctor one day" said Peggy, to no one in particular, they all seemed to be talking at the same time.

"How old is your brother, and why does he want to be a doctor" said a voice behind her. Turning round Peggy looked straight into two big blue eyes; they twinkled as he spoke, "Sorry, I couldn't help over hearing as I came through the door"

Peggy told him the story of the school getting bombed and how Harry had helped get the little boy and girl out of the rubble. He listened with great interest, and said he would like to meet Harry.

Peggy talked to him for a long time and she could see out of the corner of her eye; Pete didn't like it very much. It gave her a little thrill to think he was jealous

Matron asked them if they would like to see the rest of the work they did; now that they had finished their meal. She took them to one side and said "you may find this part of the hospital a little distressing, if at any time you do not wish to carry on, please don't be afraid to say, as I will quite understand"

She led them through a long corridor that seemed to separate them from the hospital, although they were still in the same building. Peggy began to feel a little bit apprehensive when Matron used a key to unlock the door to one of the wards.

She explained to them, that these men were suffering from mental problems all caused during the battles they had been in. The locked doors were for their own protection. Peggy stood just inside the door for a minute; she just couldn't believe it; these poor men, some of them just looked like boys. Her heart went out to them as they gathered around her, wanting nothing more than to touch her arms; her face, and even her clothes.

Their bodies were whole, but their minds empty, some talked jibberish, others spoke not at all; they just stared into space, copying other lads movements, and not even aware of it. Peggy noticed a young lad sat by himself, at the other end of the room, she went over to talk to him, he had his back facing her. His hair was almost grey, his shoulders slumped as he sat in a big armchair. She could see how thin he was, and there was a silence surrounding him. He didn't turn round even when she spoke, but somehow Peggy couldn't leave him; she wanted to see his face, so she went round his chair and stood in front of him.

Pete looked over and saw Peggy laying on the floor in a heap, he thought at first the young fellow had pushed her. Matron and a nurse quickly lifted her into a chair and pushed her head between her legs.

When she first came round all she could mutter was 'Fred', Matron looked at Pete and said, "Have you any idea what this is all about; and who is Fred."

Pete explained to Matron about Peggy's brother, and the telegram they had received from war office. She looked thoughtful, "Poor child this has been too much for her, she is probably imagining her brother could be somewhere like this"

"NO! NO! I'm not imagining it that man is our Fred, Peggy shouted. The tears began to flood from her eyes and flow down her cheeks, she was inconsolable Pete didn't know what to do.

"Have her parents got a car young man? And are they on the telephone?" Matron asked of Pete. He was in shock himself but he managed to give her a clear answer.

"No Matron they haven't got a car, they were thinking about buying one, then this blessed war broke out. But they have got a phone"

"Come we will go back to my office, it will be less stressful for Peggy and I will talk with her mother, although it will be such a shock for her, won't it? OH dear Oh dear what a mess"

Pete put his arm around Peggy and led her to Matrons room, she was still sobbing   "Oh Pete I know it was him and he didn't even recognise me, he didn't speak, his eyes seemed empty."

"I know darling but you must realise he has been through a lot of tragedy Matron says he is suffering from shell shock" When Pete told her Matron had sent for her parents, she gave a little sigh of relief. She needed her mum just now more than she had ever done in her life. Her mother had a knack of putting things in prospective.

Chapter Fifteen

Sal and Joe arrived at the hospital, both looked worried and didn't quite know what to expect, Matron explained the situation to them, and had made an appointment for them to have a word with the Doctor in charge of Fred's case.

"Of course you understand he is not known to us as Fred, we have been calling him Bill. You see when he was picked up and brought to the hospital he had no identification on him, and he was unaware of what was going on."

"Will he get his um …um…memory back?" asked Sal in an unsteady voice."It would be awful if he never knows who we are"

"Of course at this stage we cannot rule anything out, but we are quite optimistic that one day he will come out of it," he looked at Sal with a sympathetic smile, "You do realise it will take a lot of patience and loving care, but with God on our side he will come through it."

He took Sal and Joe along to the ward, explaining things as they went, the only information he had was that three soldiers, of which Bill was one; had been walking along the main road aimlessly. They had cuts and bruises all over their arms and legs.

The doctor told Joe that one of the lads had been so badly mangled they had to amputate one of his arms. Bills wounds had healed but not his mind as yet, but they were hopeful. We do know of course that they were at the battle of Casino in Italy and were flown here for treatment and to recuperate.

Sal took a deep breath before she entered the ward; her watery eyes were searching the room, darting from one lad to another, her hands twitching as she went further into the room.

"Fred oh my darling son" she whispered almost to herself, but Joe heard her and put his hand in hers, holding it tight. She went up to him quietly and looked into his eyes, they seemed lifeless. "Hello Bill," she said quietly, "and how are you today"

He looked up at her but it was obvious he thought she was just another nurse. Joe stood beside her, but the lad seemed to be upset by Joe's presence, The doctor took hold of Joe's arm and led him away saying quietly, "Don't read too much into that re-action Mr. Cheadle, after all it was men he was at war with, and who were bombing and shelling him. They accept me because of my white coat, if I was to take it off, they wouldn't trust me. Do you understand what I am trying to say?"

"Of course doctor, it makes sense to me. Tell me is there another hospital nearer to our home that could take care of him?" Unfortunately there wasn't and the doctor couldn't say how long it would be before they could have him home with them.

It was getting dark by the time they arrived home

again. Both were tired and feeling very upset. Peggy and Pete had already given the young ones their meal and a bath. They were sitting in their dressing gowns listening to Pete, who was reading them a story.

Joe thought the best thing was for them all to have an early night, it had been quite a stressful day. As Sal kissed Harry goodnight and tucked him in, he said in a quiet voice, "Was it really our Fred mum? And can I go with you next time to see him? She kissed him softly on his cheek and answered; "If it's at all possible, Harry then of course we will take you. But we shall have to ask the doctor first."

It wasn't long before Sal and Joe retired to bed, They lay in silence in each other's arms taking comfort in the warmth of each other's body. Sal had a restless night, tossing and turning, at one point she was calling Fred's name in her sleep. Joe held her close whispering comforting words in her ear, until at last she slept peacefully.

Chapter Sixteen

Six months to the very day Sal and Joe were allowed to take Fred home, they took Harry with them. Fred had been told who he really was, but was still a little nervous around Joe. Although Joe was a little hurt, he tried hard not to show it, and kept his spirits up in front of his son.

Harry and Fred were sitting in the front room together Joe and Sal were both still at work. Harry said, "It's a lovely day Fred how about we go down to the smithy and see Sam? I know he would love to see you" Fred looked at him with a blank expression on his face. Never the less he stood up and nodded in agreement, and off they went. Harry wasn't quite sure if he was doing the right thing at first. How would Fred react to the noise of the hammer on the anvil and the roar of the fire as the bellows stirred it to life.

It was too late now to turn back they were almost there. The entrance to the forge was the same as always, only Sam had changed, his back was curved and his hair almost white, he looked so tired and weary. He turned round to face them and when he saw who it was his face lit up and his tired eyes held a little sparkle.

Harry looked quickly at Fred, there were tears in his eyes, but they were tears of joy. "Sam, Oh Sam, it is so good to see you" The too men hugged one another without shame. They had so much to say to one another, poor Harry felt he was intruding.

When Sal and Joe arrived home and were told what had happened they didn't know whether to scold Harry or hug him. From that moment Fred seemed to be his normal self again.

"This calls for a celebration" said Sal, "we must have a party" as she was talking Joe came Running in all excited "Quick Sal put the wireless on listen"

"THE WAR IS OVER, THE BLOODY WAR IS OVER" He picked Sal up in his arms swinging her round. "We'll have a street party, the biggest you've ever seen"

All the neighbours pitched in together, making sandwiches and cakes, trifles and jellies, it didn't seem to matter that it was your rations you were giving, everyone gave willingly.

The streets were adorned with banners and flags, someone provided music in the evening they had a torch light procession down the main road and into a nearby park. Everyone was dancing and singing, it was such a happy time, with everyone rejoicing.

The Cheadle family arrived home tired but happy, Oh yes So happy. Sal and Joe had all their family around them once more, except for dear George.

Sal hadn't forgotten him she would take fresh flowers to his little grave in the morning, perhaps Harry would like to go with her!

As they left the graveside Harry put Sals arm through

his and said, "I still want to be a doctor mum even if the war is over, I would like to try and save little children like our George"

"Yes Harry, Our George"

Printed in the United Kingdom
by Lightning Source UK Ltd.
124031UK00001B/25-75/A